NO LONGER PROPERTY OF
Seattle Public Library
SEP 20 2016

D0471149

BRITISH COLUMBIA

CANADA

N
W E
S

SALISH
SEA

WASHINGTON STATE

◆ VANCOUVER

SEATTLE
◆

OLYMPIA
◆

WILD ORCA

For the next generations of orcas and children—especially
Hailey Renee and Liam, whose parents, Alex and
Charlotte, also sing in this book

—B. P.

In memory of Rachel Carson, who
helped us understand the sea around us

—W. M.

Henry Holt and Company, *Publishers since 1866*
Henry Holt® is a registered trademark of Macmillan Publishing Group, LLC
175 Fifth Avenue, New York, NY 10010
mackids.com

Text copyright © 2018 by Brenda Peterson
Illustrations copyright © 2018 by Wendell Minor
All rights reserved.

Library of Congress Cataloging-in-Publication Data

Names: Peterson, Brenda, author. | Minor, Wendell, illustrator.
Title: Wild orca : the oldest, wisest whale in the world /
Brenda Peterson ; paintings by Wendell Minor.
Description: First edition. | New York : Christy Ottaviano Books, Henry Holt
and Company, 2018. | Summary: Mia, her family, and friends gather in the
San Juan Islands for Orca Sing, hoping that 105-year-old Granny, the oldest orca,
will return with the pods she watches over. Includes facts about Granny and orcas.
Identifiers: LCCN 2018004250 | ISBN 9781250110695 (hardcover)
Subjects: | CYAC: Killer whale—Fiction. | Whales—Fiction. | Parental behavior in animals—Fiction.
Classification: LCC PZ7.1.P452 Wil 2018 | DDC [E]—dc23
LC record available at https://lccn.loc.gov/2018004250

Our books may be purchased in bulk for promotional, educational, or business use. Please contact your local
bookseller or the Macmillan Corporate and Premium Sales Department at (800) 221-7945 ext. 5442 or by e-mail at
MacmillanSpecialMarkets@macmillan.com.

First edition, 2018 / Design by Rebecca Syracuse
The artist used gouache watercolor on Strathmore 500 Bristol paper to create the illustrations for this book.
Printed in China by Toppan Leefung Printing Ltd., Dongguan City, Guangdong Province
1 2 3 4 5 6 7 8 9 10

WILD ORCA

THE OLDEST, WISEST WHALE IN THE WORLD

BRENDA PETERSON

PAINTINGS BY **WENDELL MINOR**

Christy Ottaviano Books

Henry Holt and Company

New York

On the longest day of summer light,
Mia waits for Granny to join them for Orca Sing.

Here in the misty and magical
San Juan Islands, people come together
to sing to the orcas.

"Will Granny and her family come
again this year?" Mia asks her mother.

"Granny might visit us." Mia's mother smiles.
"If she's not too busy."

Granny *is* busy just being 105 years old.
Granny is a great-great-grandmother.
She watches over her three families
that scientists call J, K, and L pods.

Granny was born in 1911, researchers believe,
before an iceberg sank the *Titanic*,
before our two world wars.

She swam the chilly Salish Sea
soon after the Wright brothers
flew their first airplane,
and when Model T
cars first hit the road.

Before computers and the
World Wide Web—
there was Granny.
Orcas can chat and call
on their own "whale web."

"I'm worried," Mia tells her father. "We haven't spotted Granny's J pod family for a really long time."

"That's why we've come today," her father says. "Help me drop the hydrophone so we can hear if the orcas sing with us."

All her life, Mia has listened to
Granny's family pods in her father's
Lime Kiln Point research lab. She recognizes
Granny's pods just by their whistles.

Each whale whistles a name
when greeting another.
It's called a "signature whistle."

Those rapid-fire squeaks
and screeches aren't just for talking.
Orcas can *see* underwater with sound.
They hunt salmon with sonar—
it's their superpower.

Orcas bounce their whistles
off the sea bottom and boats.
They scan for dangers—
nets, sharks, big propellers,
or kayaks coming too close.

No one in Granny's family
gets lost, thanks to her
sound maps and long memory.

Mia has memorized the
calls of many of the
orcas in Granny's family pods:
Slick, Oreo, and Spock,
Wave Walker and Surprise.

Her father hands Mia her headphones.
"Listen carefully."

People sing brightly.

Drums echo like soft heartbeats.

Thrum, *thrum*, thrum, *thrum*.

With her binoculars, Mia anxiously
scans for bright blows of orca breath.

Mia is scared, thinking about
the threats these endangered orcas face—
pollution, plastics, underwater sonar tests
that can kill whales or make them go deaf.
Sometimes orcas starve,
when salmon can't swim over big dams
to find ocean or home streams.

"Do you think the babies are
still okay?" Mia asks her mother.

"Hope so," her mother says.
But they both know that sometimes
newborn orcas don't survive
their first year.

Not long ago,
new orca calves were born—
front-page news.

Orca calves are the hope for Granny's pods.
First, Granny and her family
show the babies how
to breathe together.

Twooooosh, twoosh.
Blowholes blast out air.
Rain*blows!*
Ahhh-huuup, they breathe in.
Dive deep.

New calves are born travelers.
Sometimes Granny
swims a hundred miles a day.
She leads her family through
risky waters—hunting
from Alaska to California.

On one hunt, a young female orca got trapped onshore and stranded!

She cried out for Granny and her family.
"Eeeeeee! Eeeeeee!"

Mia's father and other islanders
protected the whale with wet blankets.
They kept her skin cool
with bucket after bucket of seawater.

At last, the high tide lifted the young
orca up off the rocks. She swam *so* fast
to Granny and her family.
All the orcas whistled her name.

On Lime Kiln Point, Mia wonders:

Is another orca stranded? Is Granny dead?

No whale whistles.
Just the *shoosh* of waves and
clank-clank of a ferryboat.

Suddenly, "*Meeeeee! Meeeee!*"
Mia hears them calling before she sees—
six orcas surfacing.
Twoosh, twoosh!
Twoooosh, twooooosh!
Twoosh! Twoosh!

Dark fins
slice through whitecaps,
heading straight toward shore.

Mia recognizes Granny's whistle.
She spots the white patch below
Granny's dorsal fin,
near a half-moon nick.

"Look," she shouts happily.
"The babies—and Granny in the lead!"

Newborn calves travel safely tucked in between their aunties and Granny.

"It's a superpod!" Mia calls.
J, K, and L pods—all visiting together.
"And there's *another* new baby!"

Near shore, family pods greet each other.
Headstands and flips.
Wild cartwheels over waves.
Orcas slapping their fins. *Ker-splash!*

Rolling and bumping one another,
orcas blow and breach.
Burp and chirp.
Spin and spyhop.
Just to peek around.

Orcas sing, too.

Their calls like tiny kittens—

"*Meewwww! Meeewwww!*"

Or rusty doors— "*Creak, creak.*"

Granny waves her huge fin at Mia. She lets out rapid-fire bleeps—a click stream.

"*Click, click, click, click!*"

Ultrasonic whistles.

"*Wheeeee! Wheeeee!*"

Granny has been singing for more than one hundred years.

Mia hopes that she, like Granny,
never stops singing.
And that the new baby orcas
will live just as long as Granny.

More about Granny and Orcas

When I began writing this book, Granny was thriving and still leading her J, K, and L family pods. Each letter stands for a distinct family group in the Southern Resident Orca community, and Granny was the matriarch of them all. But in October 2016, for the first time, Granny was not spotted swimming alongside her many generations. Researchers presumed that she had died at the astonishing age of 105. Since the 1970s, the Center for Whale Research has kept photo-identification records and family trees of Granny's pods. They estimated her age by her offspring and her "whale fingerprints," which are the dorsal fin markings unique to each orca. Whale scientists name and know every orca in these Southern Resident family pods, as each death and birth is critical to these highly endangered mammals' survival. Granny's wild orcas, now down to about 76 mammals, are the most well-studied, famous whales in the world. They swim through the Pacific Northwest waters in the film *Free Willy*. Wrongly called "killer whales," these J, K, and L pods eat only salmon.

Orca mothers and their calves rarely swim more than a few body lengths away from each other. In these matriarchal orca societies, calves stay with their mothers all their lives. Orcas must never be captured and separated from their families. One of the calves from Granny's L pod, Lolita (also known as Tokitae), was stolen from the sea in 1970 and has lived for over four decades captive inside a tiny cement tank at the Miami Seaquarium. That's like living in a bathtub your whole life. Orcas belong in the wild. They have a sophisticated language. Orcas navigate using *echolocation*—just as we use sonar, they bounce sound off objects to see underwater. Granny and older orcas know acoustic maps that lead them to food sources and away from danger.

Like humans, orcas are devoted to their families. Aunties act as midwives and attentive babysitters. Grandmothers, like Granny, actively co-parent the newborns. An orca can give birth in her early teens, but only reproduces once every four to six years—so there is a lot of mother-calf bonding in between births. Orca mothers stop reproducing in their 40s. Male orcas stay with their mothers for life. By staying close to their nurturing mothers, their life span is increased. In the wild,

orcas can live between 60 and 80 years. There were elders in addition to Granny in the J, K, and L pods. Lummi lived an estimated 98 years and Ocean Sun, born in 1928, is still alive. A *lifetime* of mothering.

You can Adopt An Orca through the Whale Museum in Friday Harbor, Washington, or follow their travels online at orcanetwork.org. Every summer solstice, Seattle's City Cantabile Choir joins islanders for Orca Sing at Lime Kiln Point State Park. Often, Granny's family pods join the singers. Interspecies concerts! Granny's legacy lives on in her family and in our celebration and conservation of these amazing wild orcas.

Waldron
Island

Orcas
Island

Shaw Island

Blakely
Island

San Juan
Island

Lime Kiln
Point
State Park

Decatur Island

Lopez
Island

Lime Kiln
Lighthouse

VANCOUVER ISLAND

OLYMPIC
PENINSULA

Pacific Ocean